The Best Pet Yet

Louise Vitellaro Tidd

Photographs by Dorothy Handelman

M

The Millbrook Press

Brookfield, Connecticut

Today is a great day for Jay.
Today he gets his first pet.
But what kind of pet will he get?
Mom, Dad, and Jay
go to the pet store to choose.

5

First Jay sees a cute brown dog.
It has a short tail and big round eyes.
Will Jay get a dog?

A dog can be a lot of fun.
This dog likes to play tug-of-war.
He pulls one way. Jay pulls back.

Jay tells Mom that
this is the pet he wants.
But Mom tells him no.

She says the dog is cute.
But it is too noisy for their home.
Jay will not get this dog.

Next Jay sees a tan-and-white cat
with bright blue eyes.
Will Jay get a cat?

A cat makes a great pet.
Jay likes to hug this cat.
He likes to pet its soft fur.

Jay tells Dad
that this is the pet he wants.
But Dad tells him no.
Dad says that cats make his eyes itch.
They make his nose run.
Jay will not get a cat.

Then Jay hears a loud HELLO.
He looks up.
A big bird is talking to him.

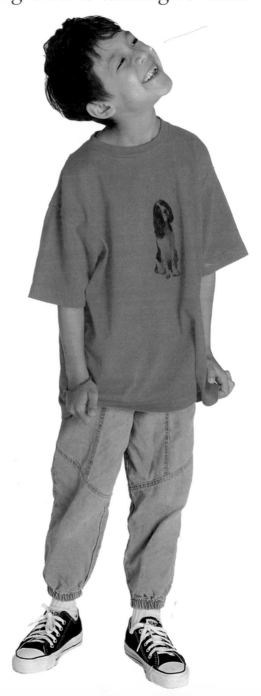

A bird might be a good pet.
Jay could teach it tricks.
He could even teach it
to say his name.

Jay tells the pet store man
that this is the pet he wants.
But the man tells him no.

He says this bird is his own pet.
It is not for sale.
Jay will not get this bird.

Jay cannot get a dog or cat.
He cannot get a bird.
Maybe he can get some fish.

Jay watches the fish swim
in their big tank.
They are nice to look at.

Mom and Dad say that fish are fine.
The pet store man says
that the fish are for sale.
Will Jay get some fish?

This time Jay says no.
He cannot play with fish.
He cannot hug them
or teach them tricks.

Jay asks the pet store man for help.
Does the man know which pet
he should get?

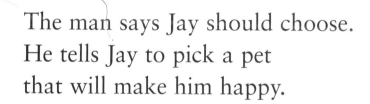

The man says Jay should choose.
He tells Jay to pick a pet
that will make him happy.

Jay thinks hard.
He wants a pet he can hug.
He wants to play with it
and teach it tricks.
So what pet should he get?

Then Jay sees a new pet.
This is the best pet yet!
It is not too noisy for Jay's home.
It does not make Dad's eyes itch.

It lives in its own cage.
It is soft and white and small.
It has long ears.
And it is for sale!

Jay is very happy.
A bunny is the best pet yet!
He can hug it and play with it
and teach it tricks.

But Jay will not get a pet today.

He will get two!

Phonic Guidelines

Use the following guidelines to help your child read the words in *The Best Pet Yet*.

Short Vowels

When two consonants surr█████ ▵wel, the sound of the vowel is usually short. This means you pronounce *a* as in apple, *e* as in egg, *i* as in igloo, *o* as in octopus, and *u* as in umbrella. Short-vowel words in this story include: *big, can, cat, Dad, dog, fun, gets, hug, Mom, not, pet, tan, tug.*

Consonant Blends

When two or more different consonants are side by side, they usually blend to make a combined sound. In this story, words with consonant blends include: *best, help, long, next, soft, swim, tank.*

Double Consonants

When two identical consonants appear side by side, one of them is silent. Double-consonant words in this story include: *pulls, tells, will.*

R-Controlled Vowels

When a vowel is followed by the letter *r*, its sound is changed by the *r*. In this story, words with *r*-controlled vowels include: *bird, for, fur, hard, war.*

Long Vowel and Silent E

If a word has a vowel and ends with an *e*, usually the vowel is long and the *e* is silent. Long vowels are pronounced the same way as their alphabet names. In this story, words with a long vowel and silent *e* include: *cage, cute, fine, home, like, make, name, nice, nose, sale.*

Double Vowels

When two vowels are side by side, usually the first vowel is long and the second vowel is silent. Double-vowel words in this story include: *day, Jay, play, sees, tail, teach.*

Diphthongs

Sometimes when two vowels (or a vowel and a consonant) are side by side, they combine to make a diphthong—a sound that is different from long or short vowel sounds. Diphthongs are: *au, aw, ew, oi, oy, ou, ow.* In this story, words with diphthongs include: *brown, new, noisy, round.*

Consonant Digraphs

Sometimes when two different consonants are side by side, they make a digraph that represents a single new sound. Consonant digraphs are: *ch, sh, th, wh.* In this story, words with digraphs include: *choose, fish, itch, short, that, they, this, what, white, with.*

Silent Consonants

Sometimes when two different consonants are side by side, one of them is silent. In this story, words with silent consonants include: *talking.*

Sight Words

Sight words are those words a reader must learn to recognize immediately—by sight—instead of by sounding them out. They occur with high frequency in easy texts. Sight words not included in the above categories are: *a, and, are, asks, at, could, go, good, great, he, hello, is, it, kind, look, no, of, own, says, the, their, to, today, too, up, very.*